zenda

A Test of Mirrors

Dedicated to:
Karlie, Sky & Ashley
Angel Girl, Johnny & Gena

Thank You to:
Bernice Sambade
Pam Amodeo
Janine Drozd
Mary Ann Wheaton
Lilly & Puddin'

zenda

A Test of Mirrors

created by
Ken Petti and John Amodeo

written with
Cassandra Westwood

Grosset & Dunlap • New York

Copyright © 2004 by Ken Petti & John Amodeo. ZENDA is a trademark of Ken Petti & John Amodeo. All rights reserved. Published by Grosset & Dunlap, a division of Penguin Young Readers Group, 345 Hudson Street, New York, New York 10014. GROSSET & DUNLAP is a trademark of Penguin Group (USA) Inc.
Printed in the U.S.A.

Library of Congress Cataloging-in-Publication Data

Petti, Ken.

A test of mirrors / created by Ken Petti and John Amodeo ; written with Cassandra Westwood.

   p. cm. — (Zenda ; 6)

Summary: On the planet Azureblue on the eve of her thirteenth birthday, Zenda finds the final three musings from her broken gazing ball and is able to attend the harana ceremony that will reveal her personal gifts and guide her life's work.

ISBN 0-448-43258-7 (pbk.)

[1. Identity—Fiction. 2. Hope—Fiction. 3. Conduct of life—Fiction. 4. Birthdays—Fiction. 5. Fantasy.] I. Amodeo, John, 1949 May 19– II. Westwood, Cassandra. III. Title. IV. Series.

PZ7.P448125Te 2004

[Fic]—dc22

2004016611

ISBN 0-448-43258-7   10 9 8 7 6 5 4 3 2 1

Contents

I'm going to turn thirteen in just a few days.

Most people can't wait to turn thirteen, right? I used to feel that way, too. But now I wish my birthday was far-off. You see, I'm running out of time.

I guess I should start from the beginning. I live on the planet Azureblue. Here, everyone is given a gazing ball when they turn twelve-and-a-half. You're supposed to study the gazing ball for six months to learn musings, special messages that help you on life's path.

I had a gazing ball, but I accidentally dropped it, and it shattered into thirteen pieces. Since then, I've been trying to get all of the pieces back. There's no sure way to find them. They appear out of nowhere in the strangest places. I've collected ten pieces of my gazing ball so far, and I've received ten musings.

But that's not enough! If I don't find all thirteen musings by my birthday, it'll be a disaster! I won't be able to attend my own private _harana_ ceremony or find out what special gift I have, a gift that will help decide what I will do for the rest of my life. It's a huge deal— and I could miss out on all of it.

I can't think about it. There's nothing I can do to make my musings come more quickly. I'll just have to get through the next few days and hope for the best. Make a wish for me, okay?

Cosmically yours,
Zenda

Celebration,
Trepidation

"Happy birthday, Camille!"

Zenda hugged her best friend, then placed a small package wrapped in yellow paper into her hands.

"Thanks, Zen," Camille said, her eyes shining.

"You've got to tell me," Zenda said. "What happened at your *harana*?"

Camille lowered her voice. "I can't tell you everything. But I'll tell you what I can."

Camille took Zenda by the arm and led her through the yard, where Camille's parents, Galen and Aponi, had set up tables covered with pale yellow and green cloths. Colorful paper butterflies had been hung from the tree branches, and now they danced in the gentle breeze.

Zenda and Camille passed Camille's parents, who were talking with Zenda's parents, Verbena and Vetiver. Aponi smiled as she saw the girls walk by.

"Don't go too far, Camille," she said.

"The rest of our guests will be here soon."

"I won't," Camille answered.

She led Zenda to a wooden bench swing hanging from the sturdy branches of a chestnut tree in the back of the yard. The two girls sat down.

"So tell me!" Zenda begged.

Camille hesitated. "Most of it's secret . . ."

"But you can tell me about your gift," Zenda urged as a bit of her impatience showed itself. "You'll be announcing it soon, anyway, won't you?"

Zenda couldn't help being excited for her friend. On the planet Azureblue, one's thirteenth birthday was an important occasion. Every girl and boy received a small, crystal sphere called a gazing ball when she or he turned twelve-and-a-half. Six months were spent studying the gazing ball, which revealed teachings called musings. At the end of the six months, the owner of the ball attended a secret ceremony called the *harana*.

At the *harana*, the girl or boy's special gift was revealed, a gift that had lain dormant for thirteen years until the ceremony. Nearly everyone on Azureblue had a gift: Some could transform musical sounds into colors and shapes; some could sense the emotions of others; some could understand the thoughts and feelings of animals. Zenda often thought that there were as many different kinds of gifts on Azureblue as there were flowers in a garden. Each one was different, and each beautiful in its own way.

One of the most revered gifts on Azureblue was the gift of *kani*, the ability to communicate with plants. Zenda's parents, Verbena and Vetiver, both had it. They used their gift to grow plants and create potions and elixirs used for healing, beauty, and aromatherapy. Their business, Azureblue Karmaceuticals, was one of the largest of its kind on the planet.

Zenda had shown signs of *kani* about a

year ago. It was rare to receive one's gift before one's thirteenth birthday, and while Zenda should have been excited, it had mostly confused and troubled her at first. She wasn't sure if she wanted *kani*, if she wanted to work with plants for the rest of her life. She had hoped her thirteenth birthday might bring a new gift with new possibilities.

Camille had hopes of her own, Zenda knew. Her friend had a fascination with insects. Since she had received her gazing ball, Camille dreamed of getting the gift of *enti*, which would allow her to communicate with bees, butterflies, and just about anything that creeped and crawled.

"Come on, Camille," Zenda whispered. "You can tell me. I promise I won't say anything."

"All right," Camille said, leaning in. Her black, curly hair had been piled up on top of her head, which was crowned with lilies of the valley. Her brown eyes, just a few shades darker than her nut-brown skin, shone with excitement. "I got it. I got *enti*!"

"You got *enti*!" Zenda realized too late that she was screaming with excitement. The girls' parents looked over at the swing and laughed.

"Try not to tell anyone else just yet, ladybug, all right?" Galen called out. "We want to save the announcement for later in the party, so everyone can find out at once."

"Sorry, Dad!" Camille called back.

"No, I'm sorry," Zenda said. "I just got so excited for you!"

Camille nodded. "I know. It's what I always wanted."

"So how do you know you have it?" Zenda asked.

"It's the strangest thing," Camille said. "After the ceremony, I started to just . . . *feel* it. Like, I knew I could do it. Marion Rose says most gifts come on strong for the first few days. I tried it out by touching a butterfly. I

6

started to get a feeling in my head. No words. Just a feeling—but I wasn't sure exactly what the butterfly was trying to tell me, you know?"

Zenda nodded. "I know. That's what the *kani* was like at first. But it gets easier."

"I hope so," Camille said.

Zenda looked down at the ground. A short line of ants scurried in front of them, headed toward the tables and chairs.

"Can you show me?" Zenda asked.

"I can try," her friend answered. Camille knelt down and put her finger in front of the ants. One crawled onto her finger, and she gingerly lifted it up. Then she closed her eyes.

She was silent for a minute. Then she opened her eyes. "It's weird. I feel like there are a million ants scurrying around in my head. But I can't really tell what the ant is saying."

"Maybe it's excited about all the food being served today," Zenda guessed. "Your mom is an amazing cook. Did she make her

7

rose petal cake?"

Camille nodded and placed the ant back on the ground. "I'll make sure to leave some for you, okay?" she told it.

"Happy birthday, Camille!"

Zenda and Camille looked down the yard to see their friend Sophia waving at them. She wore a short dress striped with the colors of the rainbow, and a crown of daisies sat atop her wild brown hair. Next to Sophia stood Willow, whose light-brown hair was pulled back in a ponytail. Her pale green dress matched the color of her eyes. The girls walked up to Zenda and Camille.

"Pretty dress," Zenda told Sophia. "Did you run out of overalls?"

Zenda wasn't being mean; Sophia wore paint-splattered overalls just about every day.

Sophia shrugged. "It's a party," she said. "I thought it would be fun for a change."

Sophia casually looked around the yard. Then her face brightened.

"Hey, it's the guys!"

A group of boys walked into the yard. Mykal, Ferris, Torin, and Darius all went to the Cobalt School for Boys together. Ferris, a tall redhead, was saying something that was making the other boys crack up. When he saw the girls, he stopped.

"Hey," he said. "Is there any cake?"

"Nice manners, Ferris," Sophia said. "How about, 'Happy birthday, Camille.' "

"Happy birthday," Ferris said. "So where's the cake?"

Mykal stepped forward. "Well, *I'd* like to wish Camille a happy birthday. How did your *harana* go?"

"Thanks, Mykal," Camille said. "It went great. I'm going to make the announcement soon."

"I hope you got what you wanted," Mykal said. His green eyes smiled through his shaggy blond hair.

He's so nice, Zenda thought. She and

Mykal had been friends since they were very young. Now Mykal helped Zenda's parents in his spare time. Zenda knew he wanted to get *kani* more than anything.

"Come on," Camille said. "Let me show you where the cake is."

Within minutes, the yard was filled with people celebrating Camille's birthday. Zenda laughed and talked with her friends. She piled her plate with watercress sandwiches, fruit salad, and rose petal cake. She was in such a good mood that she didn't cringe when Alexandra White and her mother, Magenta, arrived.

Zenda expected Alexandra to say something nasty, as she usually did. Zenda used to get embarrassed and upset when Alexandra made comments about her. Over the last few weeks, she had learned to ignore her.

But Alexandra didn't have anything mean to say today. She looked at Zenda almost shyly.

"Hi," she said quickly. Then she left for the cake table.

When everyone had eaten, Galen and Aponi brought Camille into the center of the yard. Galen called for quiet.

"My daughter Camille has something she would like to tell you," he said.

Camille smiled nervously. Zenda knew she hated speaking in front of crowds. But her voice was clear and proud.

"I received my gift today," she said. "The gift of *enti*."

Everyone clapped and cheered. Sophia and Willow ran up to Camille to congratulate her. Mykal walked to Zenda's side.

"It's just what she wanted," he said. "I hope I get what I want, too."

"You will," Zenda said. "I know it."

Mykal sighed. "I hope you're right. It must be easy, knowing your gift all along, Zenda."

Zenda didn't answer. A sudden feeling of nervousness crept over her.

Zenda had received her gazing ball, just like other girls and boys her age. But she had accidentally broken it while trying to get a look at it in advance. The ball had shattered into thirteen pieces. Ten missing pieces and ten musings had appeared to Zenda. But she was still missing three more. And her own birthday was just a week away.

She had no idea what might happen if she didn't complete her gazing ball training. She would definitely not get another gift. She might keep her *kani*—if she really had *kani*. She wasn't sure yet. Or the signs of her *kani* might fade away altogether.

Then she'd be left with no gift at all. Astral Summer was coming up, when a magical night fell on Azureblue for a whole month. All of her friends would be studying their new gifts. But she would be left out—again.

"Zenda, are you all right?" Mykal asked.

Zenda looked up at the sky. The sun was beginning to set.

"I'm fine," she said. "I'd better go see Persuaja, though. The healing center will close soon."

Mykal nodded. "I hope she gets better."

"Thanks," Zenda said. She told her parents where she was headed and said good-bye to Camille. Then she left the party.

Besides worrying about her gazing ball, Zenda had another thought on her mind. Her friend Persuaja had the gift of psychic powers. Zenda had no idea how old she was; he midnight-colored eyes seemed timeless. Persuaja lived deep in the woods, in the Hawthorn Grove, and used her powers to help others.

Persuaja had helped Zenda many times before. And now Persuaja needed help. She suffered from a mysterious illness that the healers could not diagnose. She lay in the healing center day after day, sunk into a deep sleep.

Zenda visited her friend every day. Every day, she hoped the healers would find a cure. Every day, she hoped that Persuaja would wake up. And every day, she was disappointed.

The blue-robed healers nodded as Zenda entered the healing center. They were used to her by now. She made her way to Persuaja's room, where a small fountain bubbled peacefully in the corner.

Persuaja lay on the bed. Her face looked paler than ever. Her black hair had been twisted into a long braid that reached down to her waist. Zenda sat in a chair next to the bed and grabbed Persuaja's hand.

"I'm here," she said.

Persuaja did not respond. Zenda closed her eyes and concentrated on her friend's breathing.

Get better, Zenda repeated in her mind. *Please get better.*

Soon she felt the gentle hand of a

healer on her shoulder.

"It is time to go, Zenda," said the healer, a young man with kind blue eyes.

Zenda nodded. She squeezed Persuaja's hand and left the room.

Outside the center, the sky was streaked a beautiful shade of dark purple. Each of Azureblue's four moons was beginning to rise over the horizon. They looked stunning, but Zenda couldn't enjoy their beauty.

She sat down at the base of a maple tree and took her journal out of the pouch she wore around her waist. She began to write.

Everything seems hopeless.

My birthday is one week away. But I still haven't bound the rest of the pieces to my gazing ball. I need three more pieces—three more musings. How will I do that in a week?

I don't know what will happen if I don't finish my gazing ball training. It can't be good. It's like everything I've ever dreamed of is just evaporating before my eyes.

And I'm so worried about Persuaja! She has been sick for weeks. I've asked the healers, but no one seems to know what to do to help her. I wish I could help her. But what can I do? I'm not even thirteen yet.

When Persuaja was well, she always

helped me figure out what to do.
Without her, I feel lost. I don't want
to give up hope.

But right now, I don't see any.

Cosmically yours,
Zenda

———— ∞ ————

The Wish Flower

Zenda closed her journal and put it back in her pouch. She stood up and brushed dirt from her lilac dress. Then she headed toward home.

The path back to Zenda's house followed Crystal Creek, which snaked throughout the village. Zenda loved to swim in its clear, bubbling water when the weather was warm. Suddenly thirsty, she decided to get a drink.

Zenda walked to the bank of the creek, knelt down, and scooped some of the chilly water in her hands. Her reflection stared back at her: long reddish-gold hair in a tangle of curls, large blue eyes, some rose-petal cake crumbs in the corner of her mouth. She drank the water and then straightened the crown of violets she wore on her head.

Zenda started to rise, but she stopped. Something caught her eye. In the dim light, she saw a faint purple color among the green grass of the riverbank. Quite a few species of wildflowers grew along Crystal Creek, and Zenda was pretty sure she knew them all. None were this particular shade of purple.

Zenda pushed aside the grass. Growing there, almost as if it were hiding, was a small flower. The stem couldn't have been more than three inches high. Shiny green, star-shaped leaves sprouted from the stem.

The flower itself was quite unusual. Seven long, purple petals surrounded a star-shaped, bright yellow center. The petals draped gracefully toward the ground.

"And who are you?" Zenda asked, reaching down to gently touch the flower. She thought she might be able to reach it with her *kani*, to learn something from it.

Instead, a vivid memory suddenly replayed in her mind. She was a young girl, and her grandmother, Delphina, was reading her a bedtime story. In her mind, Zenda could clearly see the cover of the book. It was called *The Wish Flower*, and the picture on the cover showed this purple flower exactly, down to its star-shaped center.

"The wish flower grows in the wild, but it is very rare," Delphina read. "And finding it in bloom is rarer still, for it blooms only one night every seven years. Those who do find the flower in bloom may ask a wish from the flower, and their wish will be granted."

The memory faded as quickly as it had appeared, and Zenda stared at the flower, her heart pounding quickly. For a full year after Delphina had read her the story, Zenda had searched the fields and woods for a wish flower. Disappointed, she had told herself that the book was just a story. It couldn't be real.

And now here it was. Zenda couldn't believe it. It probably wasn't a wish flower at all—just a flower that looked like one.

But Zenda had never seen a flower quite like it. And if it really *was* a wish flower . . .

The possibility of this overwhelmed Zenda for a moment. What a grand opportunity—to be granted a wish. There were so many things she could wish for. Her mind drifted, thinking of how she could wish for her gazing ball to be whole. Her friends and family would clap and cheer as she announced her new gift . . . a gift that she could choose for herself.

Then Zenda stopped herself. There was one person who needed a wish more than she did. It might not work, but it was worth a try. Zenda touched the wish flower again.

"I wish that Persuaja was better," she whispered. She waited for some sort of sign, like a flash of light or the chime of bells. But nothing happened.

Zenda frowned. Had it worked? The only way to find out was to go see Persuaja. But it was nearly dark now, and her parents would be getting worried. She'd go home and see if Verbena or Vetiver could get a message to the healing center.

Before Zenda rose, she touched the flower one more time. "I don't know how many wishes you give," she said. "But I'd like to find the rest of my musings. And while I'm at it, I wish I could find out why all these things have happened to me. Why can't I be just like everyone else?"

This time, the flower bud closed abruptly when Zenda stopped speaking. Zenda gave the flower one last look and then headed back to the path.

It's silly, Zenda told herself as she walked home. *I know there are flowers on Azureblue that can do all sorts of strange things. But the wish flower is just a fairy tale. I've never heard of anyone actually being granted a wish from it. And who knows if that was really a wish flower, anyway?*

By the time the fields and buildings of Azureblue Karmaceuticals came into view, Zenda had convinced herself that the wish flower was just a story. Something would have happened. Her gazing ball should have appeared out of thin air, fully formed. Something dramatic.

Still, a voice deep in her mind said, *it couldn't hurt to check on Persuaja. Just in case.*

Moonlight shone on the two-story house on top of the hill where Zenda and her parents lived. Zenda's mother had painted it in several shades of green, her favorite color. Soft light glowed through the windows; her parents must have waited for her.

Zenda started up the stairs to the front porch. At this point, Oscar, her little brown dog, usually came bounding down to greet her. But Oscar was nowhere in sight.

"What's the matter, Oscar?" Zenda called out. "Are you sleeping?"

There was no answer. Zenda shook her head and opened the door.

"You silly dog—" she began. Then she stopped.

The door slammed behind her. The room in front of her was pure white, with no windows and one door on the wall in front of her. There was no rocking chair, no fireplace, no colorful rug on the floor. It was as though she had climbed inside a big, white box.

A strange feeling crept over Zenda, making her shiver.

"Something tells me I'm not home," she said.

Two Keys

"Mom? Dad? Oscar?" Zenda called out. She knew in her heart that they were nowhere near this strange, white room, but her frightened mind prodded her to try.

There was no answer. Zenda's own voice echoed lightly in the small space. As the reality of her surroundings sank in, the truth suddenly hit her.

It was the wish flower. It had to be. The wish flower was making this happen. She didn't know why or what it had to do with her wishes.

Zenda's heart began to pound quickly. She had made too many wishes, hadn't she? That was the problem. And now something had gone wrong—horribly wrong.

Zenda turned back to the door she had entered and pulled the handle. It wouldn't budge. Next, she tried the door across the room. It was tightly locked.

Zenda started to panic. *Breathe*, she reminded herself. She took three deep breaths, one after the other, as she always did when she was scared.

Zenda got to the second breath and stopped. Her panic overtook her, and she frantically pounded on the door, then pulled on the doorknob. Nothing worked.

Zenda tried breathing again. *One . . . two . . . three.*

Stay calm, she told herself. She had been in dangerous situations before. And she had always managed to get out of them. She just had to think.

"All right," she said out loud. "What am I supposed to do?"

Immediately after speaking the words, Zenda noticed a table in a corner of the room, to the right of the door across from her. She didn't remember seeing it before. Goose bumps popped up on her arms. It didn't seem possible that she hadn't noticed the table before. Someone—or something—had made it appear.

Zenda's heart began to beat quickly

again. What was she up against? She wasn't sure. But there was only one way to find out. She cautiously approached the table.

On the tabletop sat a clay pot that held a plant and a rack of glass bottles. The plant was a thick, green stem with two large, shiny, green leaves. On top of the stem was a closed, pale green flower bud.

Zenda leaned closer and saw a sign sticking into the pot, right underneath the plant.

When the flower blooms, you'll find the key.

The key to what? The door, maybe? It was some kind of puzzle—and if she figured it out, she might find a way out of this place.

Zenda examined the bottles next, hoping to find some sort of clue. Each bottle contained a different colored, cloudy liquid that reminded Zenda of the plant food her father concocted to help their plants grow. A bottle with a bright green solution in it bore the label: "Quick Fix."

Zenda read the other labels. They were all similar. "Short Cut." "Instant Satisfaction." "Fast Acting."

Zenda had an idea of what she was supposed to do. One of the bottles of plant food would feed the plant, and the flower would bloom. But which one should she pick? They all sounded like they would do the job.

The faster she was out of this room, the better, Zenda reasoned. She chose "Fast Acting" and dumped the pink liquid inside the clay pot and around the plant. The closed bud began to grow and swell. But instead of opening, it exploded in a tiny shower of sparks. Zenda frowned.

"I guess that wasn't the right one," she mused.

To Zenda's relief, another bloom sprouted from the stem. She had another chance. She would have to get it right this time.

"Fast Acting" hadn't worked. So going fast wasn't the right solution. *I rushed the first*

time, Zenda realized. *That's what I normally do. Maybe I should be more careful this time.*

Zenda looked at the rack of bottles again, examining each one by one. This time, she noticed a bottle in the back of the rack. It held a pale blue liquid, and the label read: "Patience."

Of course! It was just like her very first musing: *Every flower blooms in its own time.* It was Zenda's impatience that had caused her to break her gazing ball in the first place.

Zenda found herself smiling. Even though she had earned that musing, she still found herself being impatient. If she had been patient, she would have chosen the right bottle the first time.

Zenda carefully picked up the bottle of Patience, uncorked it, and poured the liquid on the plant. She watched and waited as the bloom slowly unfurled to reveal thirteen pale blue petals. Cradled inside was a shiny silver key!

Zenda picked up the key. "Thank you,"

she told the plant. Then she walked to the door next to the table and tried the key. As the door swung open, Zenda hoped that she would find a way home on the other side.

She stepped into a room just like the one she had left. Once again, the door swung shut behind her. Zenda tried to open it, but as she expected, she found that she couldn't do it.

Another puzzle, Zenda thought. She took a deep breath. *I can get through this. There has to be a way out eventually.*

Just as before, there was another door on the wall across the room. But this door was locked with a chain that was held together by a large padlock. Zenda approached the door and saw that a word was engraved into the metal padlock: *Jealousy*.

Zenda's eighth musing immediately came to mind: *Jealousy is the lock that closes your mind and heart; understanding is the key that opens them.*

That had been a difficult musing to learn. When Willow first came to their village,

Zenda had been jealous of the attention she got from Camille and Mykal. Not only that, but Willow had received a gift early, too: She could communicate with animals. And Willow seemed so much better at handling her gift than Zenda was at handling her *kani*—Zenda was constantly making mistakes.

Zenda hadn't wanted to admit it at first, but she had been jealous of Willow. Mykal had helped her see the truth. He pointed out that he was just trying to make Willow feel welcome, because she had lived in so many different villages in her life. He and Camille were just being nice.

Once Zenda realized that, she got her musing. She and Willow had become friends in the last few weeks. She was glad her jealousy hadn't kept her from getting to know a good friend.

Zenda had learned her lesson about jealousy. But how was that supposed to help her open the door? She slowly looked around the room.

This time, she saw a small table appear in the center of the room. It started out as a faded image and then transformed into a solid object in front of her eyes. She gasped. How was this all happening?

Zenda took another deep breath. Everything happening was definitely weird, but she didn't seem to be in any danger. If she wanted to get through the door, she'd have to keep going.

Zenda walked to the table. On the table were four round silver boxes. Zenda looked closer. The lid of each box was a circle made of smooth, flat, white stone. Each stone bore a colorful image.

The first box Zenda looked at had a picture of her and Camille sitting side by side on her porch swing. The second box showed her and Mykal weeding the rose garden together. The third box showed her and Willow, sitting cross-legged on the floor of their school classroom. And the fourth box showed Camille, Mykal, Willow, and Zenda together, standing in the Commons Circle at the center of the village.

Zenda knew that the way to get out of the room was in one of those boxes. But which one should she pick? The box with her best friend? Or was it the box with her and Willow, to show that she and Willow were friends now?

Zenda almost picked up that box, then stopped. She didn't want to be wrong. What if she didn't get a second chance this time?

Zenda looked at the boxes again. They seemed to tell a story. Zenda had a strong relationship with all of her friends. But her jealousy of Willow had almost torn them all apart. When Zenda had learned her musing, she had realized that they were stronger together.

It must be the box with all of us, Zenda guessed. She slowly picked it up.

As soon as she lifted the box, the others vanished. There was definitely no second chance this time. Her hand trembling, Zenda opened the lid.

The box contained a silver key with a long body, straight teeth on the bottom, and a rounded top. A single word had been inscribed on the body of the key.

Understanding.

Zenda smiled. That had to be it! She brought the key to the door and inserted it into the padlock. Before she pushed the door open, she made a wish under her breath. Why not?

"I wish I was back home."

Zenda pushed open the door. The room in front of her was as black as night. She frowned.

Walking into an all-white room was one thing. But this looked, well . . . kind of scary.

Be brave, she told herself. *Keep going and you'll find a way out.*

Zenda stepped inside.

*Past
and
Future*

The door slammed shut behind her. Zenda didn't even bother to try and open it again. She knew what would happen. She took a careful step forward.

Two candles burst into flame in the center of the room. Zenda saw that they illuminated a black velvet curtain. The curtain stretched across the room, blocking her path to the door that—she hoped—was on the other side.

A thought popped into Zenda's mind. So far, the key to leaving each room had been in one of her musings. Zenda had passed through two rooms, but she had received ten musings so far. That could mean that she had to pass through eight more rooms, including this one . . . So if there *was* a door on the other side of the curtain, it probably led to another challenge.

Zenda examined the curtain, puzzled. What musing could the curtain be related to? Opening a curtain was easy enough, wasn't it?

Even if it was dark, and she had no idea what was behind it . . .

Then Zenda heard it. A long, low growl rose from behind the curtain. Zenda stopped, her heart beating wildly.

There was something behind there. Some kind of monster, maybe. It certainly didn't sound human.

Zenda looked back at the door behind her. It was still closed, of course. To go forward, she'd have to open the curtain.

The growling noise stopped. Zenda reached forward with a trembling hand. Before she could touch the curtain, the monster growled again. This time, the roar was so loud, it shook the black velvet.

Zenda jumped back. Tears sprang to her eyes. She felt paralyzed. She couldn't open the curtain. She just couldn't. She'd be stuck in this room forever.

As soon as she had the thought, she realized how silly it sounded. She had gotten through the first three challenges, hadn't she? And she had been all ready to pull open the curtain before she had heard the growl.

No, a little voice in Zenda's head told her. *Something happened before the growl. You started imagining that something scary was behind the curtain.* Then *you heard the growl. Your own fear caused this.*

And then Zenda realized what musing this challenge was about. Not long ago, on the moon Aquaria, Zenda had eaten a berry that caused dreams to come to life. One of Zenda's nightmares had become real, and Zenda had gotten rid of it by confronting her fear, facing it down. Once she had done that, she had received her sixth musing: *When you face your fears, they no longer have power over you.*

Zenda knew what she had to do. She had to open the curtain and face down whatever was there. It was the only way. She took a deep breath.

"I am not afraid," she whispered, but

her hand was trembling. She reached for the curtain again. The growl roared louder this time, reverberating in her eardrums. She wanted to run, to scream, but she held fast. She quickly pulled the curtain aside.

And found herself face to face with another Zenda!

This Zenda was a mirror image. She smiled. Then she disappeared, like a morning mist fading in the sunlight.

Zenda jumped back. Coming face to face with herself was unsettling. But a light suddenly filled the dark room, making everything seem slightly less spooky.

"I was right," Zenda said, breathing out the words. The fear had come from inside her. She had created her fear, and she was the only one who could get rid of it.

On the opposite wall, a closed door swung open. She had done it!

"The rest can't be as scary as this one," Zenda told herself. But she wasn't so sure. Still shaking, she stepped inside the next room.

This space was also dark but illuminated by candles set in sconces on the walls. Another table sat in the center of the room. Zenda stepped closer to the round, wooden table and saw that it was crowded with a variety of unusual items: A dark purple silk scarf was draped across it; glittering stones were scattered across its surface; and a large crystal ball rose from the center, balanced on top of a silver pedestal.

Zenda immediately thought of Persuaja. The psychic's cabin was filled with all kinds of items that had vaguely magical purposes. Persuaja's crystal ball had always fascinated Zenda. She knew Persuaja used the ball to see images of the future. Zenda studied the table closely. There was no clue or puzzle given. How was she supposed to open the door?

As Zenda pondered this, the crystal ball began to glow softly from within. Zenda leaned in and watched, breathless, as images began to swirl inside the globe.

Zenda made out the figure of a boy and a girl, sitting together on the banks of Crystal Creek. The girl had curly red hair, and the boy had shaggy blond hair.

Zenda gasped. The images inside the crystal ball were her and Mykal! They looked different, though—older, maybe—and Zenda realized that the ball was showing a glimpse of her future.

Zenda leaned closer, curious. She had been trying to figure out her feelings for Mykal for months now, and they confused her. She thought maybe she liked him as more than a friend. She had never had a crush on a boy before—if that's what these feelings were. She wasn't sure, and that confused her even more. And if she *did* have a crush on Mykal, well . . . would he ever feel the same way?

The figures inside the globe were talking, but Zenda couldn't make out the words. Maybe the globe would show her future with Mykal. How easy that would be. Then she could stop worrying how to act around him. She'd know what to do. Zenda strained to hear . . .

And then she pulled back. Did she *really* want to know what her future with Mykal was? She wasn't sure. She liked the way things were now. Mykal was one of her best friends. She didn't want anything to change that right now.

Zenda quickly picked up the purple scarf and draped it over the crystal ball. The light in the ball immediately went out. At the same time, the door in front of her opened.

Zenda smiled. The table had been a puzzle after all. She remembered her third musing: *The best thing about the future is that it happens one day at a time.*

Zenda knew that she could use the musing to help get back home now, too. She'd just have to face the challenges ahead of her, one at a time, and do her best.

She walked into the next room and found another table in the middle. On top of this table was a glass tank with several bugs crawling around inside. Zenda looked closer and realized they were cerulean beetles — bugs with hard, shiny shells in a bright blue color. Zenda often encountered the harmless beetle in the gardens at home. She wasn't in love with bugs the way Camille was, but she had always thought the cerulean beetle was pretty.

But Zenda noticed that one of the beetles was pure white, not blue. She frowned. Was this part of the challenge somehow?

As if to answer her question, three potted plants suddenly appeared on the table. Zenda's stomach flip-flopped. She didn't think she would ever get used to the strange magic of this place, whatever was causing it.

Once she shook off the eerie feeling, she examined the plants.

One pot contained a low-growing violet

47

with bright blue flowers. The second contained a clump of bushy green clover. And the third held a bright yellow marsh dandelion with spiky leaves. There was a small card in front of the pots. Zenda picked it up and read it.

By now you must know what to do.
Turn the pure white beetle blue.

"One of the plants must cure the beetle," Zenda said, and as soon as she had the thought, she knew what musing this challenge was about.

A few weeks ago, every girl in Zenda's class had been given an impossus caterpillar to take care of. Zenda had been nervous, unsure that she could take care of such a little creature. Her fears were realized when the caterpillar escaped and then became sick. But in the end, the caterpillar had survived to become a beautiful butterfly. And Zenda had received her tenth musing: *You can turn your*

weaknesses into strengths.

Zenda nervously bit her lip. She had help with her caterpillar from Willow and Camille and Mykal. She didn't know if she could help this beetle on her own.

She'd have to use her *kani* to figure out which plant she should feed the beetle. She'd had so much trouble with her *kani* ever since she had first gotten her gift. She'd made red roses turn blue and even caused firebrush flowers to explode.

But I've gotten better, Zenda reminded herself. She still wasn't an expert at it, but she had used her gift to get out of some tricky situations before. She'd have to try it now.

Zenda closed her eyes and touched the violet first, thinking it might be some kind of clue. If she was impatient, she realized, she might have tried feeding the violet to the beetle without using her *kani* on it first.

Zenda sent an image of the beetle to the violet. There was no response for a minute, then a startling image flashed in her mind. She saw the beetle on its back, obviously ill. She quickly took her hand away.

"Right," Zenda said. It was a good thing she hadn't used the violet. She tried the marsh dandelion next. The spiky leaves tickled her palm as she touched it.

The marsh dandelion was a happy plant, Zenda realized as soon as she touched it. Images of the sun and a blue sky filled her mind. But nothing about the beetle. Zenda frowned. Was the dandelion trying to tell her that it was okay to feed it to the beetle? She wasn't sure.

Zenda moved on to the clover. She took a few deep breaths, closed her eyes, and tried again. She sent an image of the white beetle to the clover.

Can you help? she thought, sending the words to the clover.

A peaceful, gentle feeling filled Zenda. In her mind, she saw the white beetle. The beetle slowly turned bright blue.

Zenda took her hand off the clover and smiled. This must be it!

"Thank you," she told it. Then she gently plucked one of the stems.

Zenda looked back at the tank of beetles and grimaced. She thought cerulean beetles were pretty, but she had never touched one before. The thought of sticking her hand in the tank was almost worse than the thought of opening the curtain.

You can turn your weaknesses into strengths, Zenda reminded herself. She might as well get it over with. She held her breath and stuck her hand in the tank, gently grabbing the white beetle. Then she quickly removed her hand.

The beetle tickled her palm just as the dandelion leaves had done. Zenda placed the clover stem in front of the white beetle, and the bug immediately began to munch the leaves. As Zenda watched, the top of the beetle's head turned bright blue. The blue color spread down the beetle's body until it looked like all the others.

Zenda dropped the beetle back in the tank and let out a long, relieved breath. She heard a creaking sound behind her and turned around. The door leading to the next room had swung open.

Pride filled Zenda as she walked to the door. When her *kani* worked, it felt so satisfying.

She looked through the door. Gray mist filled the room. Zenda took a step inside.

And felt herself falling!

Free Fall

Zenda screamed as she felt herself plummeting down, down as the mist swirled around her. She seemed to be falling in slow motion somehow.

Zenda flailed her arms wildly, hoping to find something to grab onto. There was nothing.

Think, Zenda told herself. *It's a challenge. There has to be some way to get out of it.*

The other challenges were all about her musings. Zenda closed her eyes and concentrated on each of her musings, one by one. There had to be one that would help her in this situation.

Help. The word stuck out in her mind. She could certainly use some help right now.

Sometimes it takes more courage to ask for help than to act alone. Her ninth musing raced through her mind.

But who was there to help her now? Was there someone out there in the mist, ready to come to her aid? It didn't seem likely, but she had to try.

"Help!" Zenda cried. "Somebody,

anybody, help me!"

The mist parted. Zenda looked down and saw what seemed to be a bottomless pit beneath her.

Before she could panic, a thick rope fell from nowhere. Zenda grabbed hold and wrapped her body around it. She sighed with relief as the falling sensation stopped.

Then she noticed a wall across from her — and an open door.

"Thanks!" she called to her unseen helper. Then she swung her body through the door.

Zenda saw a floor beneath her and jumped off the rope. The rope swung back out the door, and the door shut behind her.

She had landed in another white room. This time, small crystals of different sizes hung from strings attached to the ceiling. Zenda brushed through them to reach the door on the opposite wall. A sign above the door read: "The key to this door is Happiness." There was a small hole underneath the doorknob, where the lock should have been.

"The crystals," Zenda said out loud. "One of them must be the key to open the door. I just have to find one marked 'Happiness.'"

But as Zenda examined the crystals, she realized the task wouldn't be so easy. Inside each crystal was a tiny picture. One showed her dog, Oscar. Another showed Camille. She looked at another and saw Luna, the cloth doll that had once belonged to her grandmother, Delphina. When Zenda was sad or confused, she often confided her troubles in Luna. The colorful doll was a link to the grandmother Zenda missed so much.

These are all things that make me happy. Does that mean all of them will open the door? Something told Zenda that wasn't the way it worked. She'd have to pick one.

Zenda looked at more crystals and discovered some were more intricate than others. She found one that showed an image of her building a campfire on Aquaria when she, Camille, Mykal, and Alexandra had gotten lost. Another showed her and Willow, side by side, looking at her sick impossus caterpillar.

Zenda was confused at first. She didn't immediately associate these memories with happiness. They both showed scary and dangerous situations.

But they worked out, Zenda remembered. *I survived Aquaria. I learned how to put aside my jealousy and work with Willow. Those things made me happy.*

Still, neither one seemed like the right crystal to open the door. Zenda looked through more crystals—one contained her mother dancing; another contained her favorite dress; another showed Delphina picking flowers in a field. But none seemed right.

Finally, she came to a crystal with a smooth, mirrored surface. When Zenda looked at it, she saw her own face reflected.

"It's just me," she said.

Then she smiled.

To find happiness in life, you must first be happy with yourself.

Her second musing. Zenda knew this had to be the right crystal. The key to opening the door was being happy with herself.

Zenda tugged at the thin string and detached the crystal from the ceiling. She walked to the door and pushed the crystal through the opening underneath the doorknob.

The door swung open.

Zenda looked down and saw another bottomless pit.

"Not again," she moaned.

This time, she clearly saw the door on the other side. It was open, waiting for her. But how was she supposed to get across?

In answer to her question, a platform swung across the open space. The platform was about as long and wide as Zenda was tall. It swung from the ceiling on ropes—back and forth, back and forth. It swung in the middle of the room.

It was the only way across. Zenda would have to jump onto the moving platform. Then she'd have to jump from the platform to the door. If she fell, she'd be free-falling again—and this time, she wasn't sure if anyone would help her.

"Thorns!" Zenda cried.

Two Crowns

Zenda stood at the edge of the door, unable to move. This was scarier than the monster behind the curtain. She could *see* this challenge, and she didn't like it at all.

"Help?" she cried out tentatively, hoping that this was somehow a test of her ninth musing. "Anybody out there?"

But this time, no help appeared. Zenda knew she would have to do this on her own.

"But this is harder than anything I've ever done!" Zenda wailed.

Or was it? Zenda thought once again about how she and her friends had become lost on the wild moon, Aquaria. Zenda had found herself doing things she had never imagined she would do. She had camped out overnight, with nothing but the ground beneath her and the stars overhead. She had foraged for food. And in the end, she had crossed a deep ravine.

She had her friends to help her then. But she had done it. She had survived. And she had earned her seventh musing: *A chance not taken is an opportunity missed.*

Zenda had to try to cross the room. It was a chance she knew she had to take.

Zenda took a deep breath. The platform was pretty large, after all. It would be hard to miss. And it wasn't moving that fast . . .

"One . . . two . . . three!" Zenda jumped from the safety of the door and soared across the gap. Her flower crown slid off her head and plummeted into the abyss, but Zenda landed squarely on the platform. Her heart beat wildly in her chest.

"I did it." She didn't quite believe it. And the challenge wasn't over yet.

Zenda faced the open door. She'd have to time the jump just right in order to make it. She let the platform swing back and forth, back and forth several times until she was sure she would get it right. Then she counted off again. One . . . two . . .

"Three!" Zenda yelled. She jumped.

Her feet fell short of the door. Her arms automatically reached out, and she grabbed the bottom of the doorway just before she fell. She let out a huge breath.

I can do this, she told herself. Slowly, carefully, she pulled herself up through the open door. She collapsed on the floor, shaken and relieved, and the door shut behind her.

She rose to her feet. This room held two tall pillars. She saw a crown on top of each one.

The first crown glittered, and Zenda saw it was made of cut crystal flowers. It was absolutely beautiful. Zenda touched it, and it felt slightly cold.

The next crown was made of simple daisies. It was beautiful, too, in its own way. Zenda touched it, and the daisies began to shake, their petals raining on the floor. Zenda withdrew her hand. She knew they were reacting to her emotions leftover from the last challenge.

She still couldn't control her *kani*. Not completely. Zenda thought of how many times her *kani* had caused her flower crowns to change. Flowers had died, changed color, or sprouted angry thorns, depending on her mood. This had caused her nothing but embarrassment, but wearing flower crowns was an old tradition on Azureblue. There wasn't much she could do about it.

But a crown of crystal . . . that would never change in response to her *kani*. She could wear it and always look perfect, beautiful . . .

And she needed a crown to replace the one that she had just lost. Zenda walked back to the crystal crown. That must be why it was here—to solve Zenda's problem once and for all. She picked up the crown. It reminded her of the crystal crown her cousin Stella had given her when she visited Crystallin.

But hadn't she learned something on that planet? Zenda had tried to leave the ways of Azureblue behind her to fit in with her older cousin. But she had learned she couldn't change who she was at the core. That realization had led to her fifth musing: *Be true to who you are.*

Zenda put the crown back on the pedestal. The daisy crown might be missing petals. It might do something weird or strange when she put it on. But it was the right crown for her.

The door opened. Zenda stepped through it. Instead of another door on the opposite wall, Zenda saw two mirrors.

Zenda walked to the mirror on the left. She expected to find a reflection of herself. She did see herself, but not as she was now. She wore a beautiful silver gown that shimmered in the light. Perfect white lilies adorned her head. Her reddish-gold hair fell in perfect curls down her back. Her glowing skin was perfectly cleared.

Zenda gasped. Could that really be her? She looked so beautiful! She stared at the image for a few moments, entranced, until she remembered the other mirror.

Inside the mirror on the right was a moving image, like a memory come to life. It showed Zenda on the planet Crystallin, in the small greenhouse that her younger cousin Kaitlyn worked in. Zenda's hair was tangled, and there were smudges of dirt on her dress from working with the plants in the room. But Kaitlyn didn't seem to notice; she looked happy and enthralled with what Zenda was saying.

The image changed again. This time, Zenda saw herself at the healing center, at Persuaja's bedside. Zenda looked tired and pale. Her green dress was wrinkled. She was holding Persuaja's hand and talking softly. Her friend lay on the bed, her eyes closed.

I look terrible there, was Zenda's first reaction. She looked back at the sparkling image of herself in the silver dress. How nice she looked . . .

Mirrors reflect but people shine.

Her fourth musing popped into her head. She had received that musing on Crystallin, too. At first, she had been impressed by Stella's beauty and confidence. But even though she loved Stella, she had come to realize she wasn't always a nice person. Zenda's other cousin Kaitlyn wasn't as fashionable as Stella and wasn't outgoing at all, but her kindness made her a more beautiful person.

Zenda looked at the mirrors. In the mirror on the left, Zenda *looked* beautiful. But in the mirror on the right, she *was* beautiful. Her beauty came from the things she was doing: spending time with Kaitlyn, helping Persuaja through her illness. That was the person she wanted to be.

Zenda thought she had figured it out. But there was no door on the wall to open. No way out. She counted the challenges in her head. She had been through ten challenges. Ten musings. Shouldn't the next way out lead home? She just had to figure out how to get there.

The image in the right mirror changed again, and Zenda saw herself. Her reflection was beckoning to her with her right hand.

Then Zenda understood. She had to walk through the mirror.

"I just hope I get home," Zenda said.

Then she stepped seamlessly through the glass.

*Musings
and
Mirrors*

Zenda's body tingled as she passed through the mirror. She closed her eyes.

"Please let me be home," she whispered. "I want to see Mom and Dad. And Oscar."

Zenda's foot hit the floor, and she opened her eyes. She still wasn't home. The mirror had taken her to another white room.

Zenda could feel tears of frustration forming. It wasn't fair! She had completed all the challenges. Some had been really difficult. Wasn't she done yet?

Zenda looked around the room, hoping to spot the next challenge. To her surprise, she realized there was nothing in the room — nothing at all. Not even a door!

Zenda sank to the floor, stunned. Was this it? Had all the challenges led her here, to this place? It looked like there was no way out.

She held back her tears. It looked hopeless. Just like everything else. Persuaja would never get better. She would never find all the pieces of her gazing ball. And she would never, ever get out of this room.

Hopeless.

Then Zenda felt something move on her waist. She looked down. The movement was coming from the bag that held her journal. Zenda pulled open the bag.

A butterfly flew out. Not just any butterfly—an impossus butterfly. Its wings shimmered with all the colors of the rainbow.

The butterfly flew out and sat on Zenda's knee. Zenda remembered when her caterpillar had transformed into a butterfly. It had left her with a feeling of wonder—and hope.

Zenda had felt hopeful then—hopeful that Persuaja would get better, hopeful that she would find all the pieces of her gazing ball. But she had lost that hope after time. That's what had led her to make a wish on the flower, hadn't it?

Still, seeing the butterfly reminded her that hope never really left. She had just forgotten about it. The butterfly was telling her that there was hope for this challenge, too. She couldn't give up.

Zenda stood up. "All right," she said firmly. "There's got to be a way out of here."

As soon as Zenda spoke, a door appeared on the wall next to her.

Something else happened, too.

A faint tinkling of bells filled the air. There was a small burst of light in front of Zenda's face. A small crystal shard appeared in the air. Zenda held out her palm, and it gently floated down and landed in her hand. Green mist swirled around the shard, then faded.

"Another musing," Zenda said, her voice full of wonder.

Zenda held the eleventh piece of her gazing ball up to her face. The musing was etched onto the crystal in dark green.

Never give up, and hope will lead you to your dreams.

Zenda pressed her fingers around the piece of crystal. It was real! Now she only had two more musings to go before her gazing ball was complete. Deep down, she had always known it was possible.

Zenda carefully tucked the shard into the tiny pouch she wore around her neck, where she could keep it safe until she reunited it with the other found pieces.

Zenda looked at the open door. She had no expectations this time—just hope. She stepped through to the other side.

She found herself in a round room. This time, the walls were covered with mirrors. Curious, Zenda stepped up to the one nearest her.

Like before, the mirrors contained moving images. Zenda saw Verbena and Vetiver working in their greenhouse. Vetiver was holding a vial of purple liquid up to the light, studying it with a serious face. The vial reflected in her father's wire-rimmed glasses, and his graying hair was tied in a ponytail, as usual. Nearby, Verbena was softly stroking a green plant, her eyes closed. With her long, brown hair and slight frame, she reminded Zenda of a teenager.

Zenda smiled at the image. Her parents had been so helpful when she had lost her gazing ball, and understanding, too, even though she had made some bad mistakes. Their wisdom and advice had led her on the path to finding her musings.

Zenda moved to the next mirror and saw Camille sitting at the base of a tree trunk, examining an orange butterfly on her finger. Camille had always been there for her, even when Zenda was frustrated or grumpy. Camille was a true friend.

The next mirror showed Mykal in the rose garden, carefully pruning the branches. The look on his face clearly showed that nothing else besides the roses mattered at that moment. Quiet Mykal never said very much, but he always had sound words of advice for Zenda.

Zenda moved from mirror to mirror. There was Marion Rose, her teacher, who had guided her with so much encouragement as she had searched for the missing pieces of her gazing ball. There were her cousins, Stella and Kaitlyn, smiling and laughing in Stella's underground bedroom. There was Willow, who had been nice to Zenda even when Zenda hadn't been so friendly to her.

When she came to the next mirror, she froze. It showed Persuaja, up and walking on a moonlit night! Was she awake?

But then Zenda entered the picture, running and carrying a blue orchid. Zenda realized the mirror was showing an image of the past—the first night she had met Persuaja. Her friend had helped her so much! She knew she would not have made it through the last few months without Persuaja.

The image made Zenda pause. The

mirrors showed all different people, but they all had something in common. They had all helped Zenda grow and learn since the night she had broken her gazing ball. Each in their own way had helped Zenda find the missing pieces. She felt suddenly warm inside, knowing how many people cared about her.

She moved to the last mirror and froze again. It showed an image of a tall girl with chestnut hair in a small bedroom, reading a book.

Alexandra White? It didn't make sense.

"What has Alexandra ever done to help me?" Zenda wondered.

Acceptance

Since Zenda and Alexandra had known each other, Alexandra had gone out of her way to single out Zenda, pointing out her faults in front of everyone and laughing at her. Things had gotten much worse when Zenda had developed her *kani*. Zenda had been afraid of Alexandra for a long time, afraid to speak up for herself. She had become braver about dealing with Alexandra, but the two girls certainly weren't friends. And Alexandra still made comments about Zenda—just a little more quietly now.

Zenda watched Alexandra, fuming. It was Alexandra who had set the events in motion that had led to Zenda breaking her gazing ball. Alexandra had suggested that they sneak in at night to see their gazing balls. And when Zenda's ball had shattered, Alexandra had suggested that Zenda steal a rare and dangerous orchid from her parents that would restore the ball.

It was her fault, Zenda thought. Then she

quickly scolded herself. She had learned weeks ago that Alexandra wasn't responsible for any of her troubles. Zenda was. She had agreed to every scheme Alexandra had suggested.

Still . . . Alexandra's hurtful comments hadn't made things any easier. And sometimes she had been just plain mean, like when she threw Zenda's journal into the river on Aquaria.

No, Alexandra had been no help at all. So what was she doing in one of the mirrors?

Zenda studied the image. Alexandra was sitting back against the pillows on her bed, reading a book. The room had been painted a shade of pale, icy blue. The wooden desk, dresser, and bookshelves were painted bright white. Everything was neat and in order—the exact opposite of Zenda's room. The only thing similar were the rows and rows of books on the shelves, although Alexandra's were neatly organized, and Zenda's tended to end up in crooked piles all over her bedroom floor.

Then Alexandra's door opened, and Magenta White stepped inside. The tall woman had chestnut hair and dark eyes, and Alexandra looked very much like her.

Magenta was the headmistress of the Cobalt School for Girls. She wasn't an unfriendly woman, just strict; and while the girls respected her, few felt comfortable enough to confide in her. Thankfully, they had their teacher, Marion Rose, for that.

Magenta stood in the doorway, her arms folded across her chest. "Alexandra, must you read in bed? I have asked you time and time again to do your studying by your desk."

Alexandra sighed and climbed off the bed. "Sorry, Mother," she muttered. "It's just more comfortable that way."

"No good thinking happens lying down," Magenta said in a tired voice. Alexandra made a face that showed she had heard that phrase many times before.

Alexandra sat at her desk and opened her book again, ignoring her mother. But Magenta kept talking.

"Camille did well in her gazing ball studies," she said.

"It was a nice party," Alexandra replied.

"Don't go asking about a party again," Magenta said. "We will decide if you deserve a party once your gazing ball training is complete. I hope you receive a gift worthy of this family."

Alexandra sighed again. "What am I supposed to do? You know we don't get to decide what our gifts will be. I'll get what I'll get."

Magenta White turned and looked out the window. "I just hope it is *kani*, for your sake. It is the most important gift of all, crucial to life on Azureblue. For years, my family passed the gift of *kani* from generation to generation."

"So what happened to you?" Alexandra said under her breath.

Magenta's face reddened. "My mother

did not marry correctly. I did not make that mistake when I married."

Alexandra closed the book and rubbed her eyes. She looked weary. "I hope I get *kani*, too, if it will make you happy," she said.

"Just look at Zenda," Magenta said, turning from the window. Zenda jumped at the sound of her name. "She must have done something right to receive her *kani* so early. If Zenda can do it—"

"I can, too," Alexandra said, finishing her sentence. Zenda realized she must have heard this phrase countless times, too.

Magenta turned from the window. "Don't stay up too late," she said. Then she swiftly left the room, closing the door behind her. Alexandra opened the book again and continued to read.

Zenda was stunned. She knew Magenta was strict and cold, but never expected she would be that way with her own daughter. Magenta acted like Alexandra was some kind of disappointment to her. Alexandra might not be so nice, but she was a good student and neat and confident—lots of things that *Zenda* wasn't. Yet Magenta didn't seem to see that. She wanted Alexandra to get *kani*—just like Zenda.

"No wonder she's mean to me," Zenda said. She couldn't imagine what it would feel like to be compared to somebody else all the time.

Zenda twirled around the room, looking at the images of the people she loved—and who cared about her. They might not always have liked the things she did, but they always liked *her*. They accepted her for who she was. Even when she broke her gazing ball.

A wave of relief swept over Zenda. She had eleven musings now. She hoped she would get all thirteen before her birthday.

And if she didn't? Well, maybe it wouldn't be so bad. Verbena and Vetiver would still love her. Camille and Mykal would still be her friends. Marion Rose would still help her, and Persuaja, too, if she were able.

"It's going to be all right," she said aloud.

The mirrored walls dissolved. Zenda found herself in her own bedroom. Oscar, her dog, slept among the many pillows on her bed. A pile of clothes draped her soft, purple chair. Bottles of lotions and potions from the karmaceutical company crowded her dresser.

Zenda plucked Luna off her bed and looked at the doll's stitched-on smile.

"It's good to be home," she said. "It's good to be home!"

Peace

Zenda sat down on her bed. What had just happened? She knew it wasn't a dream — it had all felt too real for that.

"It had something to do with the wish flower," Zenda told Luna. She thought back to her wishes. She had wished to find the rest of her musings. Well, she had found one, but not all of them. She had wished to figure out why everything had happened to her. She still wasn't sure about that. And she had wished that Persuaja was better . . .

Zenda ran down the stairs. She found Verbena and Vetiver in the kitchen, sipping tea.

"I need you to do something!" she said breathlessly.

"Slow down, starshine," Vetiver said. "And when exactly did you get home? Your mother and I didn't hear you come in."

Zenda didn't know how to answer that. Her parents might understand about the wish flower, but she wasn't sure how they'd react if she told them about all of the challenges.

"I guess I was quiet," she said. "But something did happen on the way home from the healing center. I found a wish flower."

Zenda's parents looked at each other and smiled. "I remember my mother reading me that book when I was a boy," Vetiver said. "I always hoped I'd find one."

"But I *did* find one," Zenda said. "At least, I think I did. And I wished for Persuaja to get better. But I don't know if it worked or not. Can we send someone to the center to find out?"

Verbena stroked her daughter's head. "I know you're worried about Persuaja, dear. We can check in the morning."

Zenda's eyes filled with tears. "Please? I can't explain it, but I feel like something has happened."

Vetiver stood. "I'll send Niko. It won't take long."

Her father went to get Niko, one of the workers at the karmaceutical company. Many of the workers lived in cabins on the grounds.

Zenda waited on the porch for Niko to come back. Finally, she heard his horse and cart come up the path. She ran up to him. One look at Niko's face told Zenda the answer.

"Sorry," he said. "There is no change."

"Thanks, Niko," Zenda said. "I didn't mean to make you go out so late."

The dark-haired man smiled. He climbed off the wagon and patted the top of Zenda's head. "Anything for you, Zen."

Zenda said good night to her parents and went back up to her room. She began to write in her journal.

I am still not sure about what happened tonight. I thought it was the wish blower. But then why didn't any of my wishes come true?

Maybe it was a dream. Or some

other kind of flower that does weird things I don't know about. Maybe I'll never know.

And things are still pretty much where they were this afternoon. I am still missing pieces of my gazing ball. Persuaja is still sick.

But I won't give up hope. I'll try to remember my new musing. 'Never give up, and hope will lead you to your dreams.'

At least that's something.

Cosmically yours,
Zenda

On the way to school the next morning, Zenda thought about telling Camille and Mykal about her strange experience but decided against it. She did tell them about her eleventh musing.

"That's amazing, Zen!" Camille said, hugging her. "I know you're going to get your gazing ball in time."

Zenda looked at Mykal and remembered her conversation with him the day before. "I hope we all get what we want," she said, smiling. Mykal gave her a shy smile in return.

Zenda spent the first part of the morning putting the finishing touches on her project, a study of the thirteen planets in Azureblue's solar system. Then it was time for botany class with Dr. Ledger.

Normally, Zenda dreaded botany class. Not because she didn't like studying plants; she was used to that. But months ago, Dr. Ledger had made Alexandra her class partner. For the past few weeks, the girls had sat next to each other in uncomfortable silence while they tried to successfully grow a talus flower together.

Zenda filed into the lab with the other girls. Dr. Ledger looked at them over his wire-rimmed glasses.

"Today is an important day, girls," he said. "Your talus flowers should reach maturity today. We should see lots of blooms very soon!"

The girls whispered excitedly to one another. Zenda made her way to the table she shared with Alexandra. She was studying the flower and frowning.

"What if it doesn't bloom?" she asked nervously. "Will we fail?"

"I don't know," Zenda said. She realized why Alexandra sounded nervous. Her mother would probably be angry with her if she failed a class about plants.

Zenda looked at the flower. A thin, green stem rose from the clay pot in which it had been planted. Two shiny, tapering leaves grew from the center of the stem. And on top was a single, closed bud.

A cry went up on the other side of the

room. Zenda turned to see Sophia and her partner slapping hands. Their talus flower had bloomed.

"Excellent!" said Dr. Ledger. "I expect the same from all of you."

There was another cry as another talus flower burst into bloom. Zenda turned back to the plant. Now she was nervous, too.

"Maybe I could use my *kani* and see how it's feeling," she suggested.

Alexandra snorted. "Right. That'll be great if we want it to explode or sprout wings or something."

Zenda felt her face flush. Ten mean responses popped up in her mind. But she held them back. Now that she knew where Alexandra's nasty comments came from, she wasn't so angry anymore.

"Listen," Zenda said. "I know you don't like me. But I don't think you're a bad person. You're good at a lot of things. There's no reason why we have to fight all the time. I think maybe we could even be friends."

"Oh, right," Alexandra said again, but her voice was unsure. She scanned Zenda's face for signs of teasing.

"I'm serious," Zenda said. "It's too hard to be fighting all the time. I'm tired of it."

Alexandra was silent for a moment. Finally, she said, "Maybe you could try your *kani* and see what happens."

Zenda smiled. It was a start. She closed her eyes and touched the talus plant.

A strange sensation flowed through her body—like the plant was giggling! She opened her eyes and pulled back her hand. Now she was giggling, too.

"What is it?" Alexandra asked.

"I think it's happy," Zenda said.

Alexandra looked doubtful. But a moment later, the closed bud of the talus flower began to unfurl. Long, thin, yellow petals surrounded a round center. As the girls watched, the center began to spin like a

94

merry-go-round.

"We did it!" Zenda cried, and she and Alexandra hugged each other without thinking. The girls parted, and Alexandra smiled at Zenda for the first time.

"Yeah," she said. "We did it."

Suddenly, a chiming sound filled the air. A crystal shard appeared in the air. Startled, Zenda reached out and caught it. Blue mist swirled around the crystal, and Zenda watched as the mist formed the words to her twelfth musing:

Before you judge someone, imagine what the world looks like through their eyes.

"Good for you," Alexandra said. "Is that your last one?"

"No," Zenda answered. "But it's a good one!"

The Gazing
Ball

Zenda raced home after school. She found Verbena and Vetiver in the greenhouse.

"Look!" she said, taking the crystal shard from its tiny pouch. "I got another musing!"

Her parents crowded around her to get a closer look. Verbena hugged her.

"I'm so proud of you!" she gushed.

"Good work, starshine," Vetiver said. "Your mother and I were just talking about the menu for your birthday party. I was thinking of spring vegetable crepes with herb sauce and jasmine rice. Maybe some mango-pine-apple sorbet for dessert."

"That sounds yummy," she said, hugging her father. Then she frowned. "You know I might not get all my musings in time, right?"

Vetiver smiled gently. "You are going to turn thirteen with or without your gazing ball, starshine. That's still something to celebrate."

Zenda squeezed her father tightly. It was what she had known deep down, but it felt nice to hear it. Her parents would still love her, whether she completed her gazing ball or not.

That night, Zenda climbed in bed. She picked up Luna and looked into her eyes. So much had happened to her in the last few days! She wished she could tell Delphina. She missed her grandmother terribly.

"I wish you could be here for my birthday," she whispered.

Luna smiled back at her. Zenda began to feel sleepy, dreamy. A scene played in her mind.

It was the same memory she had seen on the banks of Crystal Creek. She was a young girl, and Delphina was reading a book to her. *The Wish Flower*. The scene slowly faded, and Zenda felt awake again. She picked up her journal and began to write.

I keep thinking about the wish flower. Lets say it really was a wish flower.

Did I make the right wishes?

Wishing for Persuaja to get better was a good wish. I still hope it comes true.

Wishing to find the missing pieces of my gazing ball . . . well, I've tried shortcuts before to put my gazing ball together. They never worked. There's only one way to get my musings, and that's by living and learning. I hope my thirteenth musing will come. But if it doesn't, that's okay.

My last wish was more complicated. Why me? Why did all these weird and strange things happen to me? Well, maybe the wish blower did answer that wish for me.

Going through all the challenges reminded me. I needed to experience those things for myself. Those were my lessons to learn. Things weren't always easy. But

I think maybe I did learn something from it. And maybe I'm even a better person for it. I hope so.

There's that hope again! It just won't go away.

Cosmically yours,
Zenda

Zenda closed her journal.

The sound of bells filled the air. Goose bumps rose on Zenda's arms. Could this really be it?

A piece of her gazing ball appeared in front of her face. A rainbow-colored mist swirled around it. The shard fell into her hand, and the mist formed the words of her thirteenth musing:

You can't have a rainbow without rain.

Zenda's hand was shaking. Her last musing. She had done it! She had all of the missing pieces of her gazing ball now.

Zenda walked to her dresser and opened the wooden box that held the other pieces of her gazing ball. She had carefully placed each one there after it had appeared to her. Zenda set the last piece inside the box. She was about to shut the lid when she stopped.

A warm, golden light glowed from the box. Then the light burst forth, blinding her for a second. Zenda blinked.

All thirteen pieces swirled in the air, bathed in the golden light. They seemed to dance around one another, until each found its partner, its proper place on the ball.

The light flashed again, then faded. Instead of thirteen broken pieces, a perfect crystal sphere, the size of an apple, floated in the air. Zenda held out her hands, and it gently landed in her outstretched palms.

The light faded entirely now. Zenda looked at the smooth surface of the ball and saw her own astonished face reflected back. She smiled.

"Thank you," she whispered.

The Secret
Ceremony

The next morning, Zenda showed the gazing ball to Verbena and Vetiver. To Zenda's embarrassment, they both began to cry. Zenda raced to Camille's house as soon as the family hugfest was over. She had tucked the gazing ball inside a satin pouch. She ran up the steps to Camille's porch and knocked on the door.

Camille answered. Her four-year-old sister, Lorelle, clung to Camille's green skirt.

"Hey! What's going on?" Camille asked.

Zenda held out the pouch. "I got it," she whispered.

Camille's eyes widened. "Oh, Zen. Your gazing ball? Really?"

Zenda nodded, too happy to speak. She pulled Camille and Lorelle out onto the porch. They sat on the steps. Zenda gingerly took the box from the pouch, then lifted the lid. The gazing ball glittered in the morning sunlight.

"Pretty," Lorelle cooed.

Camille gave Zenda a hug. "You did it! I always knew you would!"

"I guess I always did, too," Zenda said. "I still can't believe it though."

"I'm not even going to ask to touch it," Camille said, her face serious.

Zenda laughed. "I know. I was nervous about bringing it out. But I just had to show you!"

Zenda closed the lid of the box. "I'm so happy I get to go to my *harana*."

"That's just three days away, right?" Camille said. "Zenda, I can't wait!"

Zenda spent the next three days showing the gazing ball to anyone who would look. She had even taken it to the healing center so she could tell Persuaja about it. Worries about Persuaja still clouded her happiness about completing her gazing ball. The night before her birthday, she drifted off, dreaming of Persuaja's pale face.

She woke that morning to a happy sound.

"Happy birthday, starshine!"

Zenda sleepily opened her eyes to see Verbena and Vetiver standing over her bed. Vetiver carried a tray of food.

Zenda smiled. "It looks delicious!" she said. The tray held a stack of raspberry pancakes and honey, a bowl of fruit, and a glass of peach nectar. "Thank you!"

"You need a good breakfast before your gazing ball ceremony," Vetiver said.

Zenda suddenly felt nervous. She had no idea what the ceremony entailed. When it was over, she would find out what her special gift was. She'd been dreaming of this day for years—and now it was finally here!

Verbena sensed her nervousness. "Don't worry," she said. "You'll do just fine. I know it."

Zenda ended up sharing most of her breakfast with Oscar. Her stomach seemed to be filled with butterflies. She washed and put on a sleeveless purple dress that reached her ankles. Then she picked up her gazing ball box and headed downstairs.

Verbena and Vetiver waited by the door for her. Vetiver held a flower crown in his hands. Zenda saw that it was made of purple clover. Its fuzzy blossoms were in bloom.

"For luck," Vetiver said, placing the crown on her head. "But you won't need it. You're going to do great."

Verbena kissed her on the forehead. "Whatever happens, it's going to be a great party."

Zenda nodded. She gave Oscar one last pet. Then she headed to the Cobalt School for Girls.

The school buildings were made up of four U-shaped buildings surrounding a tall willow tree. Normally, Zenda attended classes in the Sage Building. Today she walked to a building with a lotus flower carved on the door. The building was normally used for gatherings and events, but all of the gazing ball ceremonies were held there, too.

Zenda stopped at the door, too nervous

to go inside.

A chance not taken is an opportunity missed.

Zenda smiled. Her musings just seemed to come to her when she needed them these days. She opened the door.

Pale green silk curtains covered the windows of the room. Her teacher, Marion Rose, was sitting in a circle of candles that had been arranged on the floor. There was a green silk pillow opposite her.

"Come and sit, Zenda," the teacher said, smiling.

Zenda sat on the pillow and placed the gazing ball's box on the floor in front of her. She looked into Marion Rose's smiling face and relaxed. She was glad her teacher was here with her. Marion Rose's round face and wide blue eyes matched her kind and open personality. Her teacher wore a dress the color of moss. Her long, blonde hair cascaded down her back in a tight braid.

"This will be easier than you think,"

Marion Rose said. "I just need you to speak your musings out loud, one by one. The gazing ball will do the rest."

Zenda nodded, feeling a little more confident. After all that had happened, she felt as though her musings were a part of her. Zenda took a deep breath and began.

"Every flower blooms in its own time," she said out loud.

The box holding the gazing ball opened on its own. The gazing ball floated up and out of the box and hovered in the air between her and Marion Rose.

The ball began to spin slowly. Moving images suddenly appeared inside. Zenda saw herself dropping her gazing ball on that night six months ago.

"To find happiness in life, you must first be happy with yourself."

Now the image changed, and Zenda saw herself looking into the crystal pyramid at Persuaja's cabin.

"The best thing about the future is that it happens one day at a time.

Mirrors reflect but people shine.

Be true to who you are.

When you face your fears, they no longer have power over you.

A chance not taken is an opportunity missed."

As Zenda said the musings, one by one, the gazing ball showed her how she had earned each one. She saw herself in another dimension where everyone loved her, facing a deadly yowi snake on Crystallin, being chased by her nightmare on Aquaria.

"Jealousy is the lock that closes your mind and heart; understanding is the key that opens them.

Sometimes it takes more courage to ask for help than to act alone.

You can turn your weaknesses into strengths."

The gazing ball showed her the events of

the last few days, facing the challenges of the wish flower and talking with Alexandra.

"Never give up, and hope will lead you to your dreams.

Before you judge someone, imagine what the world looks like through their eyes.

You can't have a rainbow without rain."

The last scene the gazing ball showed Zenda was an image of herself, writing in her journal. Then the scene faded. A pure white light filled the gazing ball. Then the light shot out of the ball, bathing Zenda in its glow.

Zenda suddenly felt as though her spirit had been yanked out of her body. She saw herself swirling in a whirlpool of color—every color in the world, it seemed, including some colors that seemed not to be of this world. She swam, weightless, in a sea of red and blue, green and yellow, white and silver, black and brown. She felt like she could float like this forever . . .

Then, abruptly, she was back in her

body. The light from the gazing ball had faded, and it rested in its box once more. Marion Rose smiled at her.

"You did well, Zenda," she said.

"I'm—I'm not sure what happened," Zenda replied.

"Once you successfully recited your musings, the gazing ball revealed your special gift to you," the teacher explained.

Zenda frowned. "But I didn't see any gift. Just a bunch of colors."

Marion Rose raised an eyebrow. "Sometimes, the aspects of the gift hit full force right after the ceremony," she said. "Other times, they take a while to reveal themselves. Do you feel any different?"

Zenda thought about it. "Not really." Then something occurred to her. "What about my *kani*? Would I know if I still have it?"

Marion Rose motioned toward the small pond in the corner. "You can find out."

Zenda stood up and walked to the pond,

where several lotus flowers bloomed in the water. She reached out and touched one of them. Nothing happened at first, but then a peaceful, flowing feeling filled her, and she knew she was communicating with the plant.

"It's still here," Zenda said, and she found out she was relieved. She would have missed her *kani*. The realization surprised her a bit. A few months ago, she would have been glad to give up her *kani*. Now she was glad she had it.

"I'm happy," Marion Rose said. "You have used your gift well. But there may be another gift in store for you. It is rare, but people who receive their gifts early often receive an additional gift at the *harana*. Just be patient. Remember, every flower blooms in its own time."

Zenda smiled. "You're right," she said, but she was feeling a little disappointed. She was happy to have her *kani*, but a small part of her still hoped for something different, something new.

Marion Rose stood up and hugged her. "Well done, Zenda. I will see you at the party."

Zenda picked up her gazing ball and stepped out into the sunlight. As she walked away from the school, she passed many people on the path. Today was a free day, and most Azureans liked to spend it shopping in the marketplace.

To her surprise, she saw Camille coming toward her. "I had to find out how it went," her friend said. "Did you get another gift?"

"I don't think so," Zenda began, and then her head suddenly felt light. She closed her eyes. When she opened them, she noticed a soft orange glow around Camille's body. Zenda gasped.

"Camille, you're glowing!" Zenda exclaimed.

"Thanks," she said. "I used some chamomile lotion this morning."

"No, I mean you're *really* glowing.

Orange! Don't you see it?" The glow was becoming brighter now.

Camille shook her head. "Zenda, what are you talking about?"

Zenda looked around at the other people on the path. A woman carrying a basket of apples was surrounded by a pale green light. A little boy ran past her, chasing a squirrel. He was glowing bright blue.

Zenda was reminded of the whirling colors she had experienced during her gazing ball ceremony. "I'll be right back!" she told Camille.

Zenda raced back to the Lotus Building. She found Marion Rose extinguishing the candles in the room, humming softly to herself. The teacher had a soft pink glow around her body. She looked up when Zenda burst in.

"I'm seeing colors!" Zenda cried.

"Everywhere?" Marion Rose asked. "Or just certain places?"

Zenda thought about it. "Just people.

Everyone's glowing."

Marion Rose grinned. "Oh, Zenda, you have aura sight! How awesome for you."

"Aura sight?" Zenda had heard of it, but she wasn't sure what it was.

Marion Rose nodded. "Everyone has an aura. Kind of a force field around them that shows how their spirit is feeling. People with aura sight can actually see auras. They can tell what a person's emotional state is just by looking at them."

Zenda let the words sink in. Aura sight! She had never even thought she might get such a gift.

"It will calm down in a few days," Marion Rose said. "You'll learn how to control it better eventually."

"I've got to tell Camille! And Mykal! And Mom and Dad!" Zenda said, practically bursting with excitement.

Then she remembered one person she wanted to tell most of all.

"Tell my parents I'll be a little late for the party," Zenda said. "I've got to go see Persuaja!"

Aura Sickness

Zenda ran to the healing center. Everyone she passed on the way was glowing. The beautiful colors she saw everywhere were almost overwhelming. Marion Rose had said that the colors could reveal a person's emotional state, but Zenda had no idea what they all meant. Maybe that would come later.

When she got to the healing center, she saw that all of the healers had gentle blue auras that matched the robes they wore almost exactly.

One of the healers, a young woman with almond-colored skin and long, dark hair, went to see if Persuaja was able to receive visitors. As Zenda waited, she wondered why she was in such a hurry to tell Persuaja about her gift. Her friend probably couldn't hear her, anyway.

But maybe she can, Zenda thought. *She's helped me so much. I wouldn't have my gift without her.*

The healer came back and led Zenda to

Persuaja's room. The psychic lay on the bed as usual, her breath rising and falling slowly as she slept deeply.

"Persuaja, you'll never guess—" Zenda began. Then she stopped. "That's strange." Persuaja wasn't glowing at all.

"What do you mean?" asked the healer. "What's strange?"

Zenda felt suddenly embarrassed. "I had my gazing ball ceremony this morning, and I found out I have aura sight. Everyone else I see has an aura. But not Persuaja. I'm probably just not doing it right."

The healer looked excited. "Wait here."

She came back a few moments later with another healer, an older woman with white hair. She looked at Zenda. "You have aura sight?"

Zenda nodded. "I just got it. But I don't see one on Persuaja."

The healer held out her hand. "My name is Pei," she said. "My next question is going to sound a bit odd. Has your friend done any interdimensional traveling recently? It's very rare, but—"

"Yes!" Zenda said. "She got trapped in a crystal pyramid. Why? Does that mean something?"

"I am surprised we didn't think of it," Pei said. "She must have aura sickness!" She turned to the younger healer. "Fetch one of the aura healers right away."

The younger healer nodded and healer left.

"I don't understand," Zenda said.

"Aura sickness is very rare," said Pei. "It is only found in people who were born on the planet Muroz. When the aura is lost, the body cannot function. We did not even think to check her aura. We only do that in cases of mental or emotional illness."

"Is there a cure?" Zenda asked.

Before Pei could answer, the aura healer came in. She was a dark-skinned woman with a halo of curly brown hair around her head and big, calm eyes. She wore a pale pink robe. She studied Persuaja for a moment.

"The girl is right," she said. "It's aura sickness." She turned to Zenda. "My name's Raina. Good work. I hear it's your first day with aura sight?"

Zenda nodded. "What does it mean? Will she get better?"

The aura healer frowned. "We need some elixir of pearl flower, but we don't stock it. We don't often get people from Muroz in this village."

"Persuaja didn't know what planet she was from," Zenda explained. Then she remembered something. "We carry elixir of pearl flower at the karmacy! Verbena exports it to Muroz. I never knew why."

"Then go get some," Raina said.

"Right!" Zenda said.

Then she ran.

Endings
and
Beginnings

When Zenda arrived home, she saw that people had already gathered on the lawn in front of her house. Camille stood by the gate, waiting for her.

"Where did you go?" she asked. "You've got to tell me all about the ceremony!"

"I will!" Zenda said. "I promise! But I've got to find my parents. It's important."

Before she rushed off, she shoved her gazing ball into Camille's hands. "Please watch this for me, okay?"

"I'll be careful!" Camille called after her as she ran off, but her voice sounded nervous.

Zenda kept running. She waved at Marion Rose, Mykal and his Great Aunt Tess, and Camille's parents. Everyone's auras were glowing brightly, and she felt dizzy for a moment. But she tried to stay focused. She found Verbena and Vetiver at a long table, setting out platters of delicate crepes covered with a pale green sauce and bowls of rice speckled with herbs.

Vetiver smiled when he saw her. "Marion Rose told us you'd be late. Is everything all right?"

"It's Persuaja," Zenda said, trying to catch her breath. "They found out what's wrong with her. She needs elixir of pearl flower to get better."

"Aura sickness?" Verbena said, surprised. "But almost no one gets that here on Azureblue."

"I'll explain later," Zenda said. "Can I please get some elixir?"

Vetiver nodded. "We could send Niko with it."

"I want to do it!" Zenda said quickly.

Verbena grinned. "I think she's probably faster than Niko's horse today. Follow me, Zenda."

Zenda's mother led her through the grounds to the long, low building where the karmaceutical's products were stored. Rows and rows of shelves stretched out as far as Zenda could see. But Verbena knew exactly where to go. She flitted down an aisle in that graceful way of hers and came back holding a small, round bottle filled with a milky white liquid.

"Do what you need to do," Verbena said, handing her the bottle. "There will still be a party here when you get back."

Zenda thanked her mother and ran back to the healing center. She found Raina and Pei at Persuaja's bedside. Raina grinned when she saw Zenda.

"I told you she'd be fast," Raina said. Then she took the bottle from Zenda.

"It usually works immediately," she said. "Although recovery will take some time."

Raina dropped three drops of the elixir on Persuaja's lips. Then she stood back.

"Focus, Zenda," she said. "You should see it."

Zenda didn't know what Raina meant at first. She watched Persuaja, hoping for some sign of change. Nothing happened.

Then Zenda noticed it. A faint yellow glow appeared at the very edges of Persuaja's body. It was barely visible, but she saw it.

"I think it's working," Zenda whispered.

Persuaja slowly opened her eyes. She saw Zenda and smiled faintly.

"Hello, Zenda," she said.

Zenda fought back tears of happiness. "Hello," she said. She took Persuaja's hand and squeezed it.

Persuaja tried to sit up, but Raina gently pushed her back down. "Not yet," she said. "Your aura's still regenerating. We need to keep giving you the pearl flower elixir every few hours. You'll be good as new in a couple of days."

"Thank you," Persuaja said.

"Thank your friend here," Raina said. "She spotted the aura sickness. And it's her first day with aura sight, too."

Zenda blushed. "I didn't know it was aura sickness," she said. "Raina knew what to do."

127

Raina and Pei exchanged glances and nodded to each other.

"We'll leave you alone for a minute," Raina said. "Then you've got to go, Zenda. Persuaja needs to recover."

"All right," Zenda said. She took her seat next to Persuaja.

"I'm so glad you're better," Zenda said. "I made a wish on a wish flower. At least I think it was a wish flower. Anyway, it worked."

"Maybe it worked," Persuaja said. "And maybe it didn't. Either way, I seem to be better."

"Yes," Zenda said, glad to see Persuaja's mysterious ways hadn't been affected by her illness.

"I must tell you something, Zenda," Persuaja said. "That night, when we first met, I saw that you would help me in an important way. I did not tell you. I did not want you to carry that burden. But you have helped me, and I am grateful."

"And you've helped me, too," Zenda said.

"I got all of the missing pieces of my gazing ball. And I got another gift. I couldn't have done all that without you."

Raina stuck her head in the doorway. "All right, Zenda," she said. "Time to go."

Zenda squeezed Persuaja's hand. "I'll see you tomorrow," she promised.

"I will look forward to it," Persuaja said. "And, Zenda, do not allow any worries to cloud your mind this afternoon. Enjoy your party."

"Okay," Zenda replied. What was there to worry about now? Everything had turned out just as it was supposed to. She couldn't be happier.

Zenda stopped to say good-bye to Raina on the way out.

"Thank you so much," she told the aura healer. "Let me know if you need any more elixir of pearl flower."

"You're welcome," Raina said. "It was a pleasure to meet you. And I guess we'll be seeing more of each other at school."

"What do you mean?" Zenda asked.

"I teach aura sight at the Aurora Academy," Raina said, grinning.

"That's great!" Zenda replied. "I guess I'll have a *kani* teacher, too?"

Raina frowned. "You're the girl with the *kani*? And you have aura sight, too? I hope you've got a lot of energy."

"What do you mean?" Zenda asked. Raina's tone worried her.

"Nothing," Raina said quickly. "Not a lot of people study two gifts at once, that's all. But I'm sure you can handle it."

Raina's remarks were a little unsettling. But Zenda remembered Persuaja's advice. She wouldn't let any worries cloud her mind. Not today, anyway.

Zenda walked back home at a more normal pace. With each step, she noticed what a mess she was. There were dirt stains on her dress from when she had brushed up against trees and rocks on the path. Her hair was tangled, and her crown of clovers felt wilted.

She smiled in spite of it. *Mirrors reflect but people shine.* And today, she felt like a shining star.

By the time she got back to the party, word had gotten around about Zenda's gift and Persuaja's illness. Everyone gathered around her to find out what had happened.

"Persuaja woke up," Zenda said proudly. "She's going to be fine."

"That's my starshine," Vetiver said. Everyone clapped.

Zenda looked around at her friends and family and beamed. Everyone she loved was there: Verbena and Vetiver, Camille, Mykal, Sophia, Willow, Marion Rose, and even Mykal's crazy friends from the Cobalt School for Boys. Everyone's aura was glowing soft orange.

I hope that means they're happy, Zenda thought. *I know I am.*

The birthday party lasted until nightfall.

Verbena and Vetiver had decorated all of the tables with purple cloths, ribbons, and flowers. Zenda stuffed herself with crepes and sweet sorbet. Some of the karmacy workers brought out instruments—guitars and percussion—and began to play music. Zenda and her friends danced until the stars came out.

The end of the night found Zenda sitting with Mykal and Camille on her front porch. Oscar was curled up on her lap. Zenda finally had a chance to tell them all about her adventure with the wish flower.

"That's amazing," Camille said. "I'm glad everything worked out."

Mykal shook his head. "The strangest things happen to you, Zenda."

Zenda laughed. "They do. But maybe that's over now, now that my gazing ball is put together."

Mykal's green eyes twinkled. "Or maybe it's just beginning."

Zenda finally went to bed, happy and

exhausted. Before going to sleep, she wrote in her journal.

———⦓⦔———

Today was the best day ever!

Six months ago, when I broke my gazing ball, I thought things would never get better. But everything has worked out. I am so happy!

And I love my new gift. Aura sight is an amazing thing. I'll be glad when I can control it better. Right now Oscar's aura is pale blue. It's a little weird to see auras wherever you go!

Raina's comment does worry me a little. Is it so hard to have two gifts? I guess I will find out soon enough. School starts up in a month. I guess I'll have to learn how to use both my gifts there.

Thank goodness for the Astral Summer. I used to miss the daylight during the month. Its a little strange to have night all the time. But it will be nice to just relax and meditate for a while. The last six months have been crazy! I'm sure the Astral Summer will be nice and calm . . .

Unless Mykal's right, and things are just going to get stranger. But that couldn't happen.

Could it?

I guess I will find out!

Cosmically yours,
Zenda